This book should be returne~ ~~ ~~~~~~~~~~~~~~~~~~~~
Lancashire County Library on ~~~~~~~~~~~~~~~~~~~

Lancashire County Library,
County Hall Complex,
1st floor Christ Church Precinct,
Preston, PR1 8XJ

www.lancashire.gov.uk/libraries

LL1(A)

~~been specially adapted for developing~~

in conjunction with a **Reading Consultant.**

Special thanks to
Rachel Elliot

ORCHARD BOOKS

This story published in Great Britain in 2011 by Orchard Books
This Early Reader edition published in 2017 by The Watts Publishing Group

1 3 5 7 9 10 8 6 4 2

© 2017 Rainbow Magic Limited.
© 2017 HIT Entertainment Limited.
Illustrations © Orchard Books 2017

HIT entertainment

A CIP catalogue record for this book is available from the British Library.

ISBN 978 1 40834 575 7

Printed in China

MIX
Paper from
responsible sources
FSC® C104740
www.fsc.org

The paper and board used in this book are made from wood from responsible sources.

Orchard Books
An imprint of Hachette Children's Group
Part of The Watts Publishing Group Limited
Carmelite House, 50 Victoria Embankment, London EC4Y 0DZ

An Hachette UK Company
www.hachette.co.uk
www.hachettechildrens.co.uk

Catherine
the Fashion
Princess Fairy

Daisy Meadows

ORCHARD

www.rainbowmagic.co.uk

Jack Frost's Ice Castle

Throne Room

Grand City Gallery

The Yellow Room

Contents

Story One
The Priceless Earring

Chapter One

Fashionable Fairy Friend!

One sunny Saturday, best friends Rachel Walker and Kirsty Tate were standing in a crowd outside a beautiful palace. The girls were visiting the city for the weekend with Kirsty's parents and they were waiting to meet

a family friend, Bee, when
she had finished work. Bee
was a fashion stylist and was
inside the palace at that very
moment!

Kirsty smiled up at the palace.
"It must be fantastic to help the
princesses decide what to wear
every day," she said.

"Definitely!" agreed Rachel,
linking arms with Kirsty.

Everyone loved the three
princesses who lived in the palace,
but the youngest – Princess Edie
– was the girls' favourite!

"It's very different from the Fairyland Palace, isn't it?" Kirsty whispered.

Rachel smiled, thinking of the beautiful pink palace where Queen Titania and King Oberon lived. The girls had been special friends of Fairyland for a long time!

"I hope that we get to see the Fairyland Palace again soon," said Rachel.

"You may see it sooner than you think," said a silvery voice.

The girls jumped in surprise.

A pretty little fairy had
appeared on the gate of the
palace! She was wearing a
flowing green dress with a
matching hat. Glossy brown
hair coiled over her shoulder.

"Hello!" she said. "I'm Catherine
the Fashion Princess Fairy!"

"Hi, Catherine," said Kirsty.
"What are you doing here?"

"I've come to find you," said Catherine. "There's a problem in Fairyland – please will you help?"

"Of course we will," said Rachel at once. "But there are people everywhere! How can we be magicked to Fairyland?"

Kirsty looked around and smiled. "I've got an idea,"

she said, pointing to a large postbox nearby. "Let's slip behind there. We'll be hidden from sight!"

Catherine fluttered into Rachel's backpack and the friends darted behind the postbox. Catherine waved her wand and a ribbon of green sparkles appeared. Rachel and Kirsty felt delicate wings appear on their backs as they shrank to fairy size!

Chapter Two

Trouble in the Tower

A few moments later the girls opened their eyes. They were standing in a room filled with beautiful clothes and sparkling accessories!

"We're in the Fairyland Palace," Catherine explained, "and this is my fashion collection!"

"It's amazing!" gasped the girls, looking all around.

"It's my job to make sure that princesses everywhere always look fabulous and behave perfectly at all royal functions," she continued, but then her little face fell.

"Princess Grace is going to make an important speech in a few days' time. I need to help her look and sound her best. But someone has stolen my most precious belongings!"

Rachel and Kirsty each took one of Catherine's hands. "Tell us what happened," said Rachel.

"Queen Titania looked in her Seeing Pool," Catherine told them. "She saw that some goblins had crept in here and taken my three objects!"

"Oh, no!" said Kirsty.

"What are the objects?"
Rachel asked.

Catherine led them over to
a dressing table with three
drawers in it.

"The priceless earring belongs
in this drawer," she said. "It

makes sure that all princesses' outfits are perfect." Catherine opened the second empty drawer. "This is where the ornamental shoe should be," she went on. "It makes sure that princesses are on time for their royal functions."

Kirsty opened the third drawer. "What belongs in here?" she asked.

"The jewelled clutch bag," Catherine said. "It gives princesses the confidence to make wonderful speeches."

Rachel frowned. "What will happen if Jack Frost and his goblins keep the magical objects?"

Catherine's head drooped. "Jack Frost will possess all my fashion princess magic," she said, her eyes filling with tears.

"And that means that all royal events in Fairyland and the human world are at risk!"

Rachel looked determined. "Then we must find your objects as fast as we can!" she said.

They decided to find out how the goblins got into the palace.

The three fairies left the chamber and fluttered up a narrow staircase to a turret.

Kirsty gasped. "Look!" she cried, spotting three large pieces of material on the floor.

"Those are parachutes," said Rachel. "That's how the goblins got into the palace!"

"But how did they get out?" asked Catherine.

Kirsty's eyes opened wide. "Oh my goodness," she cried. "I think the goblins are still in the palace!"

"We'll just have to search the palace until we find those goblins," said Rachel determinedly.

After a few minutes of looking, the friends heard some squawks coming from the cloakroom by the entrance hall.

Catherine tiptoed towards the door, followed by Rachel and Kirsty. Together, they carefully pushed the door open. Inside, three goblins were prancing around in front of a large silver mirror.

"They've got my magical objects!" Catherine whispered.

Rachel and Kirsty saw that one goblin had a pearl earring dangling from his left ear.

Another was holding up a
glittering shoe, and the third
had a jewelled clutch bag
tucked under his arm.

The goblins spotted the girls!
"Run away!" they shouted,
diving for the open window.

Two of the goblins managed to get out of the window, but Rachel and Kirsty grabbed the third.

As the goblin slid back into the room, Catherine leaned towards him and took the earring from his ear.

"This magical earring belongs to me," explained Catherine.

"Jack Frost still has the shoe and bag," screeched the goblin. "You'll never find them!"

Before anyone could stop him, he hurled himself out of the window and was gone.

"At least I have my pearl
earring back," said Catherine,
holding it up in delight.
"Thanks to you, princesses
in both the human and fairy
worlds will be able to put
together perfect outfits."

"And I promise we'll find the
other two objects," said Kirsty,

hugging Catherine.

Catherine smiled. "Thank you," she said. "But for now, it's time for you to return to the human world."

Moments later the girls were human-sized again and standing behind the red postbox!

"There you are, girls!" said Mrs Tate as they stepped out from behind the postbox. Bee had just arrived.

"I'm so sorry I'm late!" she said. "Everything went wrong when I was dressing Princess Edie today. But at the last minute, the whole outfit came together."

"Thank goodness we found the earring in time!" Rachel whispered to Kirsty.

"Now," said Bee, smiling. "Time to see the sights of the city!"

Rachel and Kirsty shared excited smiles. They knew that they had two more objects to find for Catherine, but right now it was time to explore!

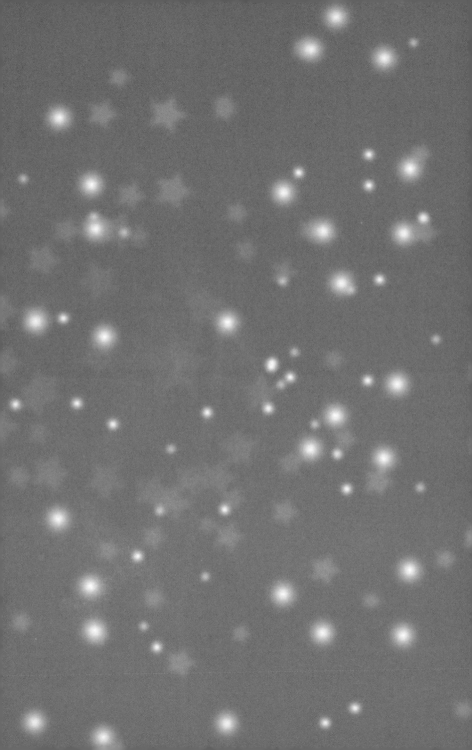

Story Two

The Ornamental Shoe

Chapter One

A Surprising Day Out

Rachel and Kirsty woke up early the next morning. They were staying in a pretty yellow room in Bee's house.

"I wonder what we're doing today," said Kirsty as the bedroom door opened and Mrs Tate bustled in.

"Morning, girls!" she said. "Bee has got tickets for a very special royal gallery opening today. Princess Edie will be there!"

"Really?" Kirsty exclaimed, leaping out of bed. "That's amazing!"

Everyone quickly got dressed and had breakfast. Then they all got on the bus that would take them to the art gallery.

When they arrived at the gallery the reception hall was filled with important-looking people, all wearing their best clothes.

Bee showed the girls a small red curtain on the wall, with a gold tassel hanging beside it. "There's a special plaque behind the curtain," she explained. "The princess will open the curtain and declare the gallery officially open!"

Bee and Kirsty's mum and dad went to look around the gallery. Suddenly, Catherine

the Fashion Princess Fairy appeared! She fluttered into Kirsty's bag and the girls went over to a quiet corner so they could talk to her properly.

"I'm so glad I've found you," she said, looking anxious.

"Jack Frost has been boasting that he's hidden my other two objects here in the human world. Please will you help me look for them?"

"Of course!" the girls cried at once.

Just then, the chatter of the crowd died down. The girls turned around and saw a worried-looking man

hurrying to stand beside the curtain.

"Ahem, excuse me, ladies and gentlemen," he said. "I'm very sorry to announce that Princess Edie has been delayed."

"This is all because of Jack Frost, isn't it?" Kirsty asked.

Catherine nodded. "It's because the ornamental shoe is missing," she explained. "Without it, no princess will ever be on time for a royal function again!"

Shoe Sighting

People started to get restless
and some boys on a school trip
began to mess around. The
friends stared at two of the boys
as they scampered through a
door at the far end of the hall.

"Hey, that boy had a green
nose!" Rachel exclaimed.

"Goblins!" said Kirsty.

"We have to follow them!" cried Rachel. "We can't let them spoil the gallery opening."

"Find a place to hide," Catherine said in a determined voice. "I'll turn you into fairies!"

The girls hid under a table covered in a white tablecloth. Catherine waved her wand and the girls changed into tiny fairies!

"Come on!" cried Catherine. "Let's catch those naughty goblins."

The girls followed the Fashion Princess Fairy as she flew up above the heads of the other guests towards the door the goblins had gone through. But the door was tightly shut!

"Let's squeeze through the keyhole," said Kirsty.

The tiny fairies squeezed through the keyhole and found themselves in a long gallery with a smooth, shiny floor.

The fairies saw the goblins at the far end of the narrow gallery, sliding along the slippery floor and shrieking with laughter.

"I've got an idea!" shouted the biggest goblin. "Let's see how fast the shoe will go!"

He pulled off his backpack
and tipped it upside down. Out
fell a tiny shoe that sparkled
with miniature diamonds.

"Ready, steady, GO!" shouted
the goblin. He pushed the shoe
as hard as he could, and it shot
along the long, polished floor
so fast that it was just a blur.

Catherine let out a
horrified squeak. "That's my
ornamental shoe – and they're
going to break it!"

Chapter Three

Goblin Games

Suddenly, a second, smaller goblin snatched the shoe. "Jack Frost told us to hide this silly shoe!" he squawked.

The goblins stomped off towards the exit door and eventually stopped beside a large sculpture in the shape

of a vase. It was green on the
outside and bright orange on
the inside. The smaller goblin
dropped the ornamental shoe
into the vase sculpture with an
echoing *THUNK*. Then the
goblins all walked off.

Rachel, Kirsty and Catherine flew over to the large vase. Catherine swooped down into it, with Kirsty behind her. But before Rachel could follow them in, she heard a furious yell. The goblins had spotted them!

The second goblin leaped towards the vase and turned it upside down. Kirsty, Catherine and the shoe were trapped!

"Let them go!" Rachel exclaimed, hovering in front of the naughty goblins.

The second
goblin gave
a mean grin.
"You're not
going to trick
me this time,"
he said. "I'm
too clever!"

Rachel's heart
was pounding, but she had
to stay calm.

"Prove how clever you are,
then," she said. "I'll ask you
one question, and you have
to get it right."

The goblin agreed.

"What colour is the inside of the vase?" asked Rachel.

The goblin laughed. "Easy!" he said. "It was orange."

Rachel shook her head.

"I think it was blue," she said.

The goblin scowled furiously. "You're wrong!" he squawked. "Look!" He lifted the vase and held it out to her. "See?" he said. "Orange! I told you so!"

Catherine and Kirsty zoomed out of the vase. Catherine was carrying the sparkling shoe!

"You're the stupidest goblin ever!" hollered the bigger goblin. "What on earth are we going to tell Jack Frost now?"

The green fiends slunk away, squabbling noisily.

Catherine smiled and waved her wand. In the blink of an eye, the girls had changed back to human size.

"I have to return the shoe to Fairyland," Catherine said. "But as soon as I hear any news about the jewelled clutch bag, I'll come and find you."

Rachel and Kirsty waved and then slipped back into the main hall. Just then, Princess Edie walked into the gallery!

She was wearing a swishy
daisy-print dress. She stepped
up beside the velvet curtain.

"I'm delighted to declare
this gallery officially ... open!"
Princess Edie said. She pulled
on the tassel and the curtain
opened to reveal the plaque.

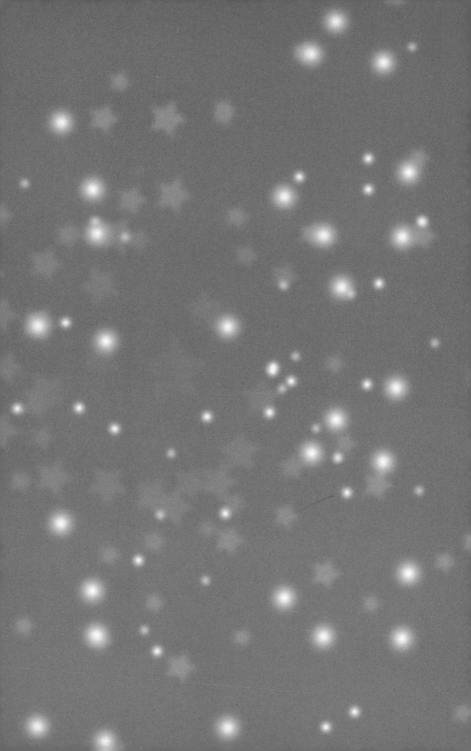

Story Three
The Jewelled Clutch Bag

Chapter One

A Midnight Adventure

Kirsty woke up with a start. It was the middle of the night. "Rachel?" she whispered. "Are you awake?"

"Yes!" Rachel replied at once. The girls heard a tinkling sound, then out of the darkness came a golden spark of light.

The girls
watched in
delight as
Catherine the
Fashion Princess
Fairy appeared!
  "Oh, girls, I'm
so sorry for waking
you up," she said in a
breathless voice. "But I've
just had a visit from a
friendly owl. He said that he
was flying over the goblin
village when he saw a goblin
making a speech."

The girls exchanged a puzzled glance. "Did the owl listen to the speech?" Kirsty asked.

Catherine nodded. "The goblin was making speeches about everything! So I think he has my jewelled clutch bag. It gives people the confidence to make speeches. Will you come to the goblin village and help me try to get it back?"

"Yes, of course," Rachel said, jumping out of bed.

"The goblin village will be very cold," said Kirsty

thoughtfully. "I think we all need to be wrapped up in something warm."

"Good idea!" said Catherine, waving her wand. A sparkling ribbon of fairy dust wrapped around the girls. They were now wearing warm coats, with thick scarves and hats pulled down low. Catherine had a white, fluffy hat and a long coat to match.

She waved her wand again
and suddenly they were
standing in the goblin village!

The girls and Catherine headed
towards the village square.
They saw that it was packed
with goblins … but for once,
they were completely silent!

A short goblin was standing on top of a box in the centre of the square. "And another thing," he was saying in a loud voice. "Being green is very unusual. It isn't like being blue or purple or red or yellow …"

"He's using magic," said Catherine, frowning. "He's got my jewelled clutch bag! It gives him the magical power to make speeches that everyone wants to hear."

Neither Kirsty nor Rachel
could move. The magic was
affecting them!

"STOP!" someone roared. The
speaking goblin disappeared
from view and the clutch bag
fell to the ground.

The magic stopped working
and the girls rushed forwards.
When they reached the box
where the goblin had been
standing, they stopped in shock.
There was Jack Frost!

Chapter Two

Into the Ice Castle

Jack Frost was shouting at the goblin. "You were supposed to hide that bag, you green fool!" he bellowed.

Kirsty tried to grab the bag, but Jack Frost picked it up and stormed off up a winding path that led to the Ice Castle.

"He's going home," said Kirsty. "Let's follow him!"

The girls hurried after Jack Frost as quickly as they could, with Catherine fluttering behind them. Ahead of them, Jack Frost reached the Ice Castle and burst through the door, slamming it shut behind him.

"We're so wrapped up, I think we could pass for goblins. Shall we try to get in through the front door?" suggested Rachel.

Kirsty nodded and the girls walked up to the Ice Castle,

with Catherine tucked behind
them. Rachel knocked on
the door and a goblin guard
opened it.

"What do you want?" he
said crossly.

"We've come to say goodnight to Jack Frost," said Kirsty. The guard glared at her, but then opened the door. Catherine gently tapped Rachel and Kirsty with her wand, and in a flash they felt wings appear on their backs.

Now they had to find Jack Frost!

The friends flew through chilly halls and echoing chambers until eventually they heard Jack Frost's voice.

"I think he's outside, at the very top of the castle," said Rachel. "Come on!"

They swooped out of the window and up to the battlements. They saw Jack Frost strutting up and down. On either side of him were rows of goblin guards. They were all listening carefully to him.

"Of course, everyone knows that I am much more interesting than any silly princess," Jack Frost was saying. He was carrying the jewelled clutch bag.

Catherine waved her wand and gave herself, Rachel and Kirsty a pair of fluffy earmuffs each. "We can't risk falling under the spell of

Jack Frost's speech!" she said.

Rachel and Kirsty flew towards Jack Frost. But he turned and saw them out of the corner of his eye. "Fairies!" he yelled. "Stop them!"

In a flash, Kirsty swooped up above Jack Frost's head. "Catch me if you can!" she shouted. Jack Frost stretched his arms up to grab her, and the clutch bag dropped to the ground!

Chapter Three

Magic in the Morning

Catherine swooped down and seized the clutch bag. Then she zoomed back up to join Rachel and Kirsty.

Jack Frost and his goblins were all jumping into the air, trying to reach the fairies.

"The clutch bag belongs to

Catherine," Rachel called down to them.

"And it's coming back to the palace with me," Catherine added.

She waved her wand, leaving a trail of sparkling fairy dust. Before the girls could blink, they were back in Catherine's tower chamber!

Catherine let out a long sigh of relief and walked over to her dressing table. She opened the third drawer and put the jewelled clutch bag inside.

"Thanks to you both, my precious objects are back where they belong!" she said.

The friends shared a big hug. "Now Princess Grace will look fantastic, arrive on time and give a wonderful speech," said Catherine. "Thank you for everything you've done, girls. Without you, this event would have been a disaster."

"It's been so much fun helping you!" said Kirsty.

"Now, I need to help Princess Grace get ready for her speech," smiled Catherine.

"And we should go back to Bee's house and get some sleep," said Rachel.

Catherine waved her wand and the girls found themselves back at home in their pyjamas, tucked into their warm beds.

The girls were so tired that they fell asleep straight away, and slept until morning!

"Wakey wakey!" called Mr Tate through the door.

Laughing, Rachel and Kirsty hopped out of bed. But when Rachel looked in the mirror, she got a big surprise!

"Kirsty, look!" she exclaimed. The mirror shimmered and a picture appeared. Princess Grace was standing among a crowd of smiling fairies. Catherine was also standing nearby, and as the girls watched, she turned and winked at them.

"I'm so happy that we were able to help her!" smiled Rachel.

"It's lovely being friends with the fairies," Kirsty said. "We're the luckiest girls in the world!"

The End

**If you enjoyed this story,
you may want to read**

Holly the
Christmas Fairy
Early Reader

Here's how the story begins ...

It was the Christmas holidays
and best friends Rachel
Walker and Kirsty Tate were at
Rachel's house.

"Only three days to go until
Christmas!" smiled Kirsty,
playing with her golden locket.

Both girls wore magical lockets. They had been a present from their very special friends, the Rainbow Magic fairies!

Mrs Walker came into the room. "Hello, girls! We're going to choose a Christmas tree later. Do you want to fetch the decorations from the garage?"

The girls ran to get the decorations. But as Rachel reached up for a box her locket burst open, scattering fairy dust everywhere!

"Kirsty!" Rachel cried as

both girls began to grow small. "We're on our way to Fairyland!"

When the girls landed by the Fairyland Palace a few moments later, Queen Titania came towards them. "Our magic made your locket open," she said. "I'm afraid we need your help again!"

Read
*Holly the Christmas Fairy
Early Reader*
to find out
what happens next!

Meet the first Rainbow Magic fairies

Ruby
the Red Fairy
Daisy Meadows

Amber
the Orange Fairy
Daisy Meadows

Saffron
the Yellow Fairy
Daisy Meadows

Fern
the Green Fairy
Daisy Meadows

Sky
the Blue Fairy
Daisy Meadows

Izzy
the Indigo Fairy
Daisy Meadows

Heather
the Violet Fairy
Daisy Meadows

Can you find one with your name?
There's a fairy book for everyone at
www.rainbowmagicbooks.co.uk

Let the magic begin!

Become a

Rainbow Magic

fairy friend and be the first to
see sneak peeks of new books.

There are lots of special offers and exclusive
competitions to win sparkly
Rainbow Magic prizes.

Sign up today at
www.rainbowmagicbooks.co.uk